To Dance With Angels

To Dance With Angels

*A Story to be Read and Enjoyed
throughout the Year*

Arthur C. Morton

**All Rights Reserved
This work is registered with a copyright
witness**

Cover painting by T. H. Gomillion
Interior illustrations by Lisa Maria Green
© 2017 **Arthur C. Morton**
All rights reserved.

ISBN-13: 9780999512401
ISBN-10: 0999512404

This book is a work of fiction. Places, events and situations in this story are purely fictional and any resemblance to actual persons, living or dead, is coincidental.

If you have a purchased this book with a dull or missing cover, you have possibly purchased an unauthorized or stolen book. Please immediately contact publisher advising where, when and how you purchased this book.

To Jordyn S. Rumble, to inspire her and us all to express the beauty and courage within ourselves.

*In loving memory of
James and Indiana "Mother" Morton
Elizabeth Johnson and Clifford Morton*

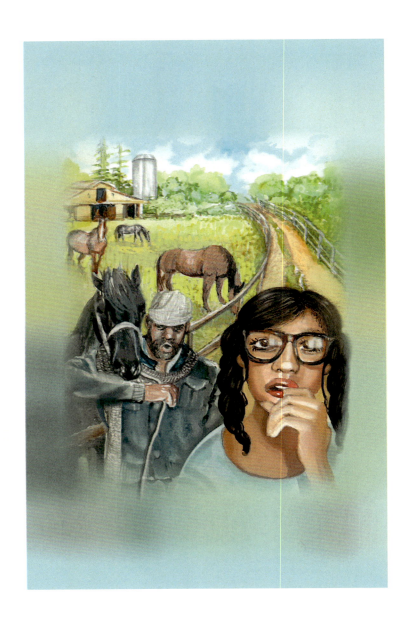

Practice, Patience, Belief

"Hey, Pop-Pop."

"Hello, Harper. What's going on with you and your friends?" He was talking to her as he leaned against the fence watching the chestnut filly prance around in the field.

"Oh, with me? You know, just stuff."

"Just stuff! Well, Harper, you look like something is bothering you."

"No, not much—except I was just thinking about wanting to dance a lead part in the Christmas play."

"Great! You have been dancing for quite a while," replied her grandfather.

"But they said I am too young and not right for the part." It seemed to everyone around Harper that she had danced every day since she first began.

"Harper, are you the best student in your class?"

"Maybe."

"Well, since you're not sure, you need to practice, practice, and practice even more, and just maybe your time will come."

"But Pop-Pop, I *am* the best dancer in my class."

"Well, keep practicing. And let me tell you something about being the best that no one pays attention to. Most often that one person is blessed with a special gift, and one day soon, you will come to know that. In the meantime, what you have to do now is continue the things you're good at: reading, writing, and arithmetic. However, you must have patience and practice your dancing faithfully if you want to stay the best. And I will say a prayer for you to get better. So get up. Be positive. Never let anyone make you feel bad about yourself. We all have gifts, and some people have very special gifts."

"OK, Pop-Pop. I will study and practice even more."

"Remember, when you're the best, they will come. When you have forgotten about them—maybe next year or maybe in ten years—they will come."

"Pop-Pop, who will come?"

"I didn't say."

"Oh, come on. Tell me. Please!"

"OK. Every once in a great while, the angels of heaven come to earth to find that one special girl, and they will give her wings to fly back to the heavens so she can dance the Dance of the Millennium."

"Pop-Pop, that's a thousand years. No way."

"A thousand years in the heavens is but a hundred earthly years. Ah, yes, my dearest. This special adventure is only given to that person blessed from her birth, and only a few people are granted such a gift because the prayers of all those who came before them were heard."

Harper thought about all that her Pop-Pop had said and grew more curious about it the longer she considered his words.

"So the Dance of the Millennium. Hmm. Maybe I will be given wings to fly into the heavens and dance."

Pop-Pop listened to Harper talking loudly to herself, and he replied, "Maybe, but do you know what's required of you?"

"Yes, Pop-Pop. Practice and more practice."

"That's right, and don't forget patience. But there is one more very special requirement: belief in yourself and in the troupe of the Heavenly Angels of the Dance. They only come when you believe. And if your spirit is right and your heart is just, then when you least expect it, one day or night, you will be awakened to go and dance the performance of your life before returning home to dance before the world."

"The entire world?"

"Yep."

"Are you sure?"

"Just as sure as I am talking to you."

"Wow! Can you help me, Pop-Pop? I want to dance the Dance of the Millennium."

"Sure I will. In fact, I think I will get you a piano."

"A piano? Why a piano, Pop-Pop?"

"Well, old folks used to say that the angels love the sound of the piano. As an old songwriter once said, 'There is nothing finer than strings changing from major to minor.'"

"I always wanted a piano of my very own to play. Thank you."

"No problem. We will start tomorrow by shopping for a piano that the angels will be happy with, OK? For now, off you go to play with your friends. Keep your head up, your back straight, and your mind as sharp as a tack."

"See you tomorrow when I get home from school."

Harper, her parents, and her grandparents all lived on the farm together in a twenty-room two-and-a-half-story old red brick and Chestnut Hill fieldstone farmhouse. Pop-Pop had grown up in this house and lived here all his life. The numerous windows had always been a stunning feature of the farmhouse, for no other homes boasted so many ways the sun could warm a family. With her parents working daily and away from the farm, Harper spent a lot of time with her grandparents.

That night before bed, Harper's grandfather made a special prayer on his old aching knees, humble and thankful for all his blessings. He began to pray the ancient prayer taught to him during one of his many visits to Ghana as a child with his parents. His prayer was that the troupe of the Heavenly Angels of the Dance would choose his granddaughter to fly way above and into the Heaven of Heavens for awhile to dance the Dance of the Millennium.

That night, while he was on his knees, his prayers and the prayers of those who came before him were heard by the Archangel Raguel, the Angel of Justice and the Angel of the Order of the heavenly dance troupe. He sent forth an angel from the troupe, whose time on earth was not long ago. She would return and take the form and name of Mrs. Minnified to be Harper's piano teacher, her guiding angel, and would prepare her to dance the Dance of the Millennium.

Unbeknownst to her grandfather, Raguel, the Angel of the Order, had set in motion the path that Harper would travel.

Tomorrow came, and Harper, getting in from school, as she always did, first checked on Grandmom and then went searching throughout the house for Pop-Pop. He was not in the house, so she knew he must be at the stable or out in the paddock schooling his horses.

"Pop-Pop, where are you?" called Harper. "You promised we would go find a piano so I can start practicing."

"Hello, Harper. I am over here in the last stall, with the filly."

"Hey, Pop-Pop. Are you ready to go find a piano?"

"Give me ten minutes. You wait in the tack room until I am ready."

Harper thought going in the tack room was like going back in time. While she waited, Harper could only imagine the fun Pop-Pop had had with his brothers and sisters, riding, showing horses, and fox hunting year in and year out. The room was filled with pictures, ribbons, trophies, and the distinct smell of leather.

"Harper, I am ready to help find that one unique piano for you, but it has to be the right one, you know."

While Pop-Pop drove Harper to the piano store in his old white pickup truck, Harper began to talk about getting a new piano. Pop-Pop remained silent, enjoying her youthful dreaming and believing.

"We're here at Minnified's Piano Store," said Pop-Pop, jumping out of the truck. Harper ran into the store and immediately started looking at the pianos. The store was filled with new and old pianos for sale. Harper strolled through the store with the biggest smile on her face at the thought of having a piano of her own, but she just couldn't make up her mind about which one to choose. She looked and looked, but she could not make up her mind.

Mrs. Minnified, the store owner, introduced herself and began to walk around the store with Harper. Mrs. Minnified had been a gifted concert pianist and dancer when she was a young lady and had played all over the world.

"So you're trying to select a piano," said Mrs. Minnified.

Harper replied, "Yes, very much so. My grandfather told me that it will help me get chosen to dance with the angels in the Dance of the Millennium. Do you know about the angels and the dance?"

Mrs. Minnified replied, "Oh yes, my dear. I do indeed. If you want that opportunity, you will need the piano that's in the far corner of the store." That piano was the one Mrs. Minnified had played as a young child when she was chosen by the Archangel Raguel and given wings to fly into the heavens, many, many years ago.

Eagerly, Harper ran to the back of the store to find the piano described to her by Mrs. Minnified. She was disappointed because it was old and dusty. What she really wanted was a new piano. Harper asked disapprovingly, "Why this one?"

"Because to play and dance with the angels, a special tone—full of brightness and quality—is needed for your heavenly audition. You want the sound of a whole orchestra to play through you. When you return to earth, your understanding of dance will be above all others because you will have danced the heavenly dance. You will then go and dance all around the world."

"That's what my Pop-Pop said. OK then. I want this piano. I will clean it up and come for piano lessons every day."

So Harper earnestly continued her lessons, learning the piano and excelling at lightning speed while advancing in her ballet and dance classes.

At the moment, though, she couldn't wait to go back to school and ballet classes to tell her classmates about her special piano and her desire to be chosen to dance with the troupe of the Heavenly Angels of the Dance. Oh, the joy she had as she told her classmates about the story told to her by her favorite grandfather.

As she continued telling the story to more students in her classroom, Little Mike called her out. "You're crazy! Dancing with angels?"

The students thought Harper had just made up the biggest story ever imagined and began laughing and calling her names, which hurt Harper's feelings very much. She felt as if the whole class was now against her. Even Mrs. Thomas, her teacher, although wanting to believe her, thought the story was quite an imaginative one—knowing, however, that Harper was one of the most creative and smartest students in her class.

Because her story was so imaginative and thus disrupted the class so much, Mrs. Thomas wanted to talk to Harper about her made-up story after school was over.

"Harper, where did you get such an outlandish story about dancing with the angels and flying off into the heavens?"

"My Pop-Pop told me that if I practice very hard and learn to be a fair and just person, then someday maybe the Heavenly Angels of the Dance will choose me from all the other children to perform the Dance of the Millennium. But most importantly, I have to believe, and I do with all my heart." Surprised by the expression on her teacher's face, Harper exclaimed, "Mrs. Thomas, you don't believe me?"

"Well, Harper, it is not that I don't believe you. I *do* believe that children should learn to treat and play with each other fairly and support their classmates and encourage them to be thinkers and dreamers. From you and your classmates will come the next leaders, thinkers, and even dancers. The whole world will benefit from your good works. So don't be disappointed when the other students laugh at you. Just remember that your special dream will require belief in yourself."

"You know, Mrs. Thomas, my Pop-Pop said the same thing."

"Well, I'm sure he is a wise and knowledgeable grandfather. Keep listening to him. I don't think he would tell you an untruth."

Feeling better about herself after talking with her teacher, Harper went to catch the school bus home. Mr. Dave, the school bus driver, who always saw Harper with her heavy book bag and her arms filled with books and sheets of music, waited for her because she was running late to get on the bus.

"What's up, Mr. Dave?"

"Not much, Harper. How was your day?"

"Mr. Dave, the kids laughed at me today because I was telling them about wanting to be a great dancer and pianist so I can dance in the heavens with the angels."

"Hey, do you think you are going to die or something?"

"No, of course not. You just get chosen to dance with the angels and learn special things, according to my grandfather, and then you return to earth to dance and play all over the world."

"Hey, that's a big dream for a small person like yourself, but I like it. So I'll tell you what. If you keep practicing and believing, I will keep driving this bus and picking you up to get you home for your music lessons and your ballet and dance classes. Is that a deal?"

"That's a deal, Mr. Dave."

"Your stop is next, so take care, and I will see you tomorrow. Try to be on time."

The Bully Squad

Harper woke up early that morning and just sat in her bed clutching her pillows. She hadn't slept well that night, because she was thinking about how the kids at school had bullied and teased her. In fact, it was now time to get up, since it was morning, but she didn't want to go back to school. Instead, at breakfast Harper complained to her grandfather, who walked her down the road to her bus stop as he did each morning for exercise.

"Harper, you're not your smiling, bubbly self this morning." Not wanting to ask her what was wrong directly, he just asked how she slept last night.

Harper replied, "I'm tired. I didn't sleep well. I kept thinking about what the kids in school said to me yesterday. Do I have to go to school?"

"Why, of course."

"They're going to bully and tease me again because I believe with all my heart in what you told me, Pop-Pop. What if I have to fight or something like that?"

"Well, fighting never resolves anything, nor is it the answer. But sometimes you have to fight for what you want, win or lose. Harper, your dream is more real than the dreams of the other kids at school. Because when they haven't taken the time to focus on what they want to do or become in life, they strike out against their classmates that have found something they want to do or become in their lives. You have decided and set your focus on dancing and playing the piano. Unfortunately, for now, some of your classmates, not having their own focus, have become troublemakers.

"So yes, they may become a bully squad, and you might have to stand up to them daily and hold your ground when they tease you, write terrible things about you, call you funny names, and even want to start fights with you.

"Harper, this is what I want you to learn to do: Keep your spirit up, walk tall, and never forget why you believe in your dream. Take a picture of your dream and tattoo it on your forehead and on your heart, because if your spirit is right and your heart is just, then the bully squad, in the long run, will see the errors of their ways and come to understand the importance of having a dream like yours.

"So finish your breakfast, because you're going to school. Learning to face and deal with your fears is a lesson we all must learn as children—and even as adults. You will begin now. I want you to repeat after me: 'I will stand tall and be just with everyone, even if they don't like me, because their dislike of me and my dreams is their problem. If we all learn to turn hate into love and love into understanding, then my dream and their dreams will be our tomorrows.'"

"Pop-Pop, that's a lot to remember."

"Harper, you can learn it, OK? That's what you will repeat to yourself daily, when the bully squad wants to make fun of you. You're becoming a big girl now, Harper, so you'll have to learn to fight your own battles, always with love and understanding."

"Pop-Pop, you know, what you said makes a lot of sense. I love you, Pop-Pop. I'm ready to walk down to the bus stop with you and catch the bus to school."

"That's my Harper. Always be bigger than your height. Let's go."

Waiting, as always, was Mr. Dave.

"Good morning, Mr. Dave."

"Good morning, Harper! How are you feeling?"

"I am feeling better now after my grandfather talked with me about not being afraid of what the kids at school would say and do to me because I want to dance with the angels."

"When you believe in something or want something very much, the journey toward achieving that thing has peaks and valleys.

When I was younger, I wanted to be a boxer and to become the best in the world."

"Really, Mr. Dave?"

"Yes, but what happened to me was that when the guys around me began to bully me and tease me, I let myself listen to them. They thought my dream was foolish and said I would never make it, even though I was a very good boxer. I gave in and listened to the bullying and the teasing. I wanted to be their friend. I wanted them to like me. So I stopped practicing. I stopped listening to my parents and the older men in the neighborhood who were telling me the right things to do. Shortly thereafter, I got in trouble and then more trouble. Time went by, and so did my dream.

"Harper, as I told you yesterday, you keep dreaming, and I'll keep driving this bus and picking you up. And if need be, I'll go up to that school and knock one or two of them out for you."

"Oh! No, Mr. Dave. Pop-Pop said fighting never resolves anything."

"Well, he is right, but I've still got a pretty good left jab if you need it." Mr. Dave winked at her while jabbing the air with his left and right hands repeatedly.

"OK."

"Please get ready. The school is just ahead. Remember my story, and never let the bullies make you lose sight of your dreams. And remember: left jab, left jab." As he spoke, he punched the air with a flurry of jabs, accidentally hitting the bus horn, which let out an unexpected blare.

"You're funny, Mr. Dave. See you after school."

Harper walked into the school, where the bully squad seemed to be waiting for her. Remembering and repeating to herself what her grandfather had told her to say daily, she began from memory, saying to herself, "I will stand tall and be just with everyone, even if they don't like me, because their dislike of me and my dreams is their problem. And if we all learn to turn hate into love and love into understanding, then my dream and their dreams will be our tomorrows."

"Harper, Harper, Harper. What crazy story will you tell us today?"

"The same one, if you want to listen," she quipped.

The bully squad, led by Little Mike and consisting of four other classmates, made fun of her that morning, but she just stood tall and walked straight ahead to her classroom.

It seemed the more she repeated what her grandfather had told her to say, the less she heard the voices of the bullies, and the better she felt inside.

With class beginning and Mrs. Thomas requiring the students to pay attention to the math problem on the blackboard, the bullying stopped for a while, but lunch and recess were coming up. Soon, Mrs. Thomas instructed the students to line up for their walk to the cafeteria. On the way to lunch and during lunch, the bully squad started picking on Harper again.

"Skinny, lying Harper with crazy stories in her head about dancing with the angels."

Wondering why kids need to bully other kids, Harper made up her mind right then that she would *never* become a bully. She would always try to be fair and understanding in all things with people, wherever they came from around the world. Lunchtime was not good, and it seemed only to encourage the bully squad, led by Little Mike, to continue their pranks and teasing.

"It hurts, their name-calling," Harper thought.

Luckily, Mrs. Thomas was keeping an eye on Little Mike and his crew. She caught them in the act, and they were sent to the principal's office. With the bully squad in the principal's office, recess was fun, even though Harper sat alone studying her music and letting her imagination carry her afar, hearing music and seeing dance movements in her head. Harper enjoyed some peace.

After lunch and back in Mrs. Thomas's classroom, the bully squad was back. They looked at Harper, and she looked at them, not once blinking her eyes, and showing no fear. In her mind, she was ready to stand tall against whatever Little Mike and his crew wanted to do to her.

"No Fear Harper is what I will nickname myself," she thought. With Pop-Pop and Mr. Dave, she was going to confront the bully squad every day until they left her alone.

When school ended, she hurried to catch her bus. The bully squad was outside staring at her, and she stared right back at them. Then, while she was looking for her bus number, she noticed that Mr. Dave was standing outside the bus for some reason.

"Mr. Dave, why are you standing outside the bus?"

"Well, I told you I've got your back, so I thought I would just let these young boys over there know that I'm watching them."

"Thank you, Mr. Dave, but I'm OK. I made up in my mind not to be afraid and to make my dream the most important thing. I'm No Fear Harper. That's my nickname."

"Good for you. Now get on the bus, and let's get you home so you can go to your dance class and music lesson."

On the bus, Mr. Dave continued to encourage her to hold on to her dream, saying, "Many things in dreams are reality; therefore, your dream will come true. Just imagine if I held on to my dreams. I don't want you to let go of your dreams, Harper. You know we both promised each other that you would keep practicing and I would keep picking you up in this old yellow school bus. Right?"

"Right. I'm going to keep practicing my dance and playing the piano, Mr. Dave."

"OK, then I'm gonna keep driving this bus and looking out for you. Your stop is next. Hurry home."

As she was getting off the bus, Harper stopped, turned around, and gave Mr. Dave the biggest smile. Then she hurried down the road home.

Her grandfather was working in the yard.

"Hey, kiddo. How was your day?"

"Hey, Pop-Pop! School was tough, but you know, I'm tougher."

"That's what I wanted to hear. Go wash up, and I'll fix you a snack before driving you to your classes."

No Fear Harper got through the first day, but the weeks and months of Little Mike and his crew tested Harper to the very core of her belief. Little Mike and his crew were always waiting at school for her, taunting, bullying, and posting unkind things around the school, and there were more cafeteria pranks, hallway taunting, and classroom digs.

Little Mike and his crew were winning by doing small silly things, such as gluing her schoolbook pages together on one day, gluing her sheet music together on another, and dropping several overripe tomatoes in her book bag on another. One day they even took their chewed-up bubble gum, once the strawberry flavor was gone, and placed it on her desk seat. Then they distracted her, and she sat on their nasty, flavorless gum. The boys were winning, it seemed, but Harper, remembering what her grandfather told her to repeat to herself, paid the boys no attention.

Another day Harper had to go to the bathroom. Unfortunately, she left her eyeglasses on her desk. The bully squad hid them from her just as the school day was ending, but Mrs. Thomas just happened to catch them in the act and made them give her the glasses. Upon Harper's return to the classroom, Mrs. Thomas said to her, "Here are your eyeglasses, Harper." Looking at Mrs. Thomas's face, Harper knew that Little Mike and his crew had just done something, but she only said thank you and packed up her books for the day.

School was over, and she headed for her bus.

Always happy to see the smiling face of Mr. Dave, she boarded the bus, but Harper complained about the silly pranks and teasing to him.

"Well, No Fear Harper also means No Tears Harper," said Mr. Dave. "I told you you'll figure it out. You're letting your guard down; you're not floating. Keep your hands up; protect the body."

"What do you mean?"

"Float like a butterfly; sting like a bee. You know like, Mr. Ali, the greatest boxer of all times. You've got to find your way, dear. Here's your stop. You think about what I said. Left jab."

Another month went by with Little Mike and his crew continuing to do things to Harper. But Little Mike and his crew went major-prank level on Harper that month. They took peanut butter and mayonnaise and mixed them with water in a squeeze bottle. As they were running past her in the hallway, they squirted her from head to toe. That was in the morning, before lunch.

No, they were not done with Harper after months of bullying. They had her mad and stressed out.

Lunch was even worse. The bully squad took their cartons of milk and poured them all over her lunch. Boy, was she mad and hurt.

Mrs. Thomas had been keeping an eye on Little Mike and his crew and again caught them in the act. They were sent to the principal's office. With the bully squad again in the principal's office, recess was again fun, even though Harper was still sitting alone, studying her music and letting her imagination carry her afar as she heard music and saw dance movements in her head. She was at peace.

After lunch and back in Mrs. Thomas's classroom, the bully squad was back as well. They looked at her, and she looked at them, not once blinking her eyes, and showing no fear.

Months of this drove her to be withdrawn from her classmates and took away the joy of going to school. "This has to stop," declared Harper. Although repeating what her Pop-Pop had told her to memorize made her feel better, she had to take it a step further. And she would—by finally confronting Little Mike and the bully squad.

"What can I do? What should I do?" Harper asked herself. She closed her eyes for a moment and cleared her head of all negative thoughts, even the thought of using her left jab—because she was a lefty, and southpaws are known to be good fighters. That wasn't Harper's style, but what could she do to stop running away or getting out of Little Mike and his crew's way?

Mr. Dave could see Harper walking toward the bus with her head hanging low and her shoulders heavy with the burden of so many school days on them.

"Hey, you know No Fear Harper means No Tears Harper."

"I know, Mr. Dave."

"Harper, it's time to fight."

"I'm not a fighter like you, Mr. Dave."

"Of course you are. Look what you have gone through these many, many months. And Christmas is coming soon too. This is your favorite time of the year, going Christmas tree cutting in the country, decorating the tree, and spending time with your family. You need to deal with this.

"I also heard you're the best in your dance class and quite a piano player as well. I've been checking up on you. You're a better fighter than me. You're stronger than me, and you're smarter than me. You can fight, girl! You've been fighting, and now it's time for you to use your left jab.

"In boxing, the jab is used to set up the opponent. You're moving around, floating, and punching with your left hand repeatedly while waiting for that opportunity to hit him with a right-hand barn burner that will drop your opponent to the mat. Knockout time. Winner. You know, there's all kinds of ways to fight back while standing tall."

"Wow, Mr. Dave. I wish I was you."

"No, never wish to be who you're not, but always wish for what you can be. I stopped wishing and dreaming, and I'm driving a bus. And that's OK for me. But for you, it's not."

"Well, I've been thinking about what I'm going to do and listening to you. I know what to do now. Thanks, Mr. Dave."

The next day, after school and before going to catch the bus home, she would confront them head on and talk, get beat up, or whatever, but that was what she was going to do.

The next day came, and like clockwork Little Mike and his crew were there, hissing and taunting, but none of that seemed to matter—not even repeating what her Pop-Pop had told her to say to herself. No, she could hear none of those things. It was time to make Mike—not Little Mike anymore, but Mike—and his crew her friends. What is fear but the absence of caring and the bravery to show it? Somehow, she would make them her friends.

When school was over, she saw Mike and his crew leaning against the wall, looking for trouble. She walked over to them, somewhat afraid, but she stood tall with her back straight, thinking only good thoughts.

"Hello, Mike. Can we talk?" she asked.

"What do you want, crazy girl with a dream? Sure, we can talk."

"I've been afraid of you and your friends, but I'm no longer afraid. If you want, you can beat me up or kick me, but I'm not going to cry. I have a dream, and I believe it with all my heart. Maybe someday soon you and your friends will have one too. I won't laugh or make fun of you if you tell me that you want to be great at something. Maybe being the greatest pitcher in baseball. I've seen you throw the ball, and you're pretty good, and you can swing that bat too. Or maybe the greatest boxer of all time. I know you can fight, and if you want to learn how to box, I'm sure my friend Mr. Dave, the bus driver, would teach you. He was pretty good in his day. I know your friends Rob, Frank, Sonny, and Al are all good at something, and belief and practice are all anyone needs."

"Hey, Harper, I like your style. You're cool. Not cool cool, but smart cool, and that's OK. I know you will do something great in life, so I'm happy that I didn't stop you. So we're gonna chill out and work on being friendly, OK?"

"That's fine with me."

"Is that fine with you, Rod, Frank, Sonny, and Al?"

"Sure," said Mike, "we're cool with that. We were beginning to feel bad about doing these things to you anyway. We're sorry, Harper."

"Well, our buses are waiting for us, so let's go home, and tomorrow let's make it a better day for all of us."

"We will," replied Mike.

"You know, Harper, I like being called Mike. My granddad is the only other person that calls me Mike."

Harper left the boys and hurried to catch the bus, where Mr. Dave was waiting.

"Hey, Harper. You seem happy."

"I am. I just confronted Mike, Rod, Frank, Sonny, and Al, the ones who were bullying me. I told them they could beat me up or kick me, but I wasn't going to cry. We began to talk, and we agreed to be friendly with each other from now on."

"Good for you. Since you're all friends now, remember, keep your left jab, and don't give away your joy by wanting to be liked."

"I won't, Mr. Dave."

"Get on the bus. This is a good day."

With smiles and relief, she hopped up the bus steps and sat in her regular first-row seat.

She could hardly wait to get home to share with her grandfather what she'd done and the outcome after finally confronting her fears. Mr. Dave and Harper talked all the way to her bus stop. They were two happy campers.

"Here's your bus stop, so hurry home and let your grandfather know."

"I sure will, and thanks again for the left jab," she said, all smiles.

She got off the bus and ran down the road. "Pop-Pop, I made friends with the boys who had been bullying me."

"You did? How did that happen?"

"I just made up my mind to stop being afraid. I told myself fear is the absence of caring and the bravery to show it. Then I walked over to them after school, standing tall with my back straight. I asked them if we could talk, and we did. I told them that they could beat me up or kick me, but I wasn't afraid, and I wasn't going to cry. I told them that I have a dream that I believe with all my heart and maybe someday soon they will have one too.

I said I wouldn't make fun of their dreams, so why make fun of mine?"

"You did? Good for you. Fear is a small thing to a giant, so always learn to be bigger than your fears. Go wash up, and I'll fix you a snack before driving you to your dance class."

Dance Class

After quickly washing up and changing into her tights, Harper ate her snack, and they were off to dance class and music lesson.

At the ballet and modern dance school, all the kids had dreams, some bigger than others. There she left the bullying and teasing behind. As at her piano lessons, it was all business. Everyone here was trying to be the best.

She enjoyed her ballet classes, from warming up on the barre to practicing all five of the traditional foot and arm positions in earnest. One could spend a lifetime perfecting them, dreaming of dancing in pointe shoes and doing steps such as the pirouette, sauté, or arabesque. "Oh, the joy of the dance," she would continually say in refrain.

Practice was hard. Every day it started with stretching exercises and then getting a good warm-up at the barre, doing pliés, relevés, ronds de jambe, battements tendus, passés, and sur le cous-de-pied, before the floor workout. Whatever the task, Harper absorbed it with glee.

The director was Mrs. E, who had danced all over the world with many different ballet and modern dance companies. Mrs. E had retired from dancing to start her school for ballet and modern dance many years ago with one goal in mind: to develop world-class students. Getting into her program required an audition and an interview. Only the best were selected. Harper had been late signing up for an audition and the interview that followed, but Mrs. E had agreed to allow her to audition and be interviewed.

At Harper's audition, Mrs. E had moved to the edge of her director's chair as she watched Harper leap and spin playfully; she was amazed to see such natural musicality and rhythm in Harper's playfulness. She got out of her director's chair and moved around the room, all the while watching Harper intensively. Mrs. E could see that Harper had "it," simply meaning a true gift from the heavens—undeveloped talent totally embodied in that slender frame. Mrs. E had wondered whether Harper in all her innocence would allow this director to develop that gift. Mrs. E also had to search deep within to know whether she had the capability of developing such a gifted talent that came along only once or twice in a director's career. So that year, which was several years ago, Harper was the last student admitted into the school's program, but one student Mrs. E would pay close attention to.

Mrs. E greeted Harper and the other students every afternoon with a hug and a warm smile while looking over the top of her glasses, making sure everyone was properly dressed and ready to practice. Knowing the routine, they all went straight to the barre and began their warm-up. Then they moved to do their normal center-floor routine, where they all developed balance, technique, and grace.

Harper's progress skyrocketed, as if she was on a trajectory all her own. She was carefully guided and developed by Mrs. E, which made some of the other dancers uncomfortable. Most of the dancers were Harper's friends. It was just a few older dancers who would always try to put her down.

By now, Harper had withstood the worst of the bully squad. Standing up to the older dancers in class was a piece of cake. Totally triumphant against the bullying, the teasing, and the put-downs, she was now entirely free to dance and focus with greater intensity on pursuing her dream.

Time passed as Harper focused on her commitment to herself to work hard and make herself strong, graceful, and tough mentally. She always remembered and repeated what her grandfather had taught her to say. She heard the voices of the bullies no longer, for she had matured and had come to realize it is how you see and think of yourself—and not what other people think and say about you—that matters. And she finally understood what it meant to have joy and a right spirit.

All her concentration now was on putting on pointe shoes, and from time to time, she thought about the story her Pop-Pop had told her when she was younger about the Heavenly Angels of the Dance, especially when she was at her piano lesson with Mrs. Minnified. Ballet and dance school was her home away from home, where she dreamed of becoming the best. And it was all worth it, because each Christmas she got to dance in the annual holiday performances, and maybe one day she would be chosen as the lead dancer for the Christmas Day performance.

Piano Lessons

Mrs. Minnified followed Harper's ballet and dance lessons closely, which seemed to encourage Harper. There was something angelic, it seemed, about Mrs. Minnified, her Pop-Pop would say all the time. All Harper knew was that she really enjoyed learning how to play the piano and talking about the future with Mrs. Minnified. The woman seemed to know a lot about things and the future. She was smart—even smarter than her old teacher, Mrs. Thomas, and Harper had thought Mrs. Thomas knew everything. Mrs. Thomas also kept a close eye on Harper's progress although Harper was no longer her student. Harper thought taking piano lessons was different from taking ballet and dance classes. Playing and learning were easier with Mrs. Minnified's help and instruction on her old piano all cleaned and tuned up.

Mrs. Minnified would always say to Harper that she had to learn to hear and to play as if she had a whole orchestra in her head, thereby allowing the total sound of the piano to flow through her body. And when she gained this understanding of and possessed this passion for the music, she would finally be able to create the magic, beauty, and greatness required for the Dance of the Millennium. Hearing this from Mrs. Minnified every day made Harper believe even more in herself and her ability to achieve such a lofty goal. As she practiced on that old piano, the brightness and clarity of the tone and sound drove her crazily forward, searching, sometimes coming close and then floating away just as quickly as she heard it.

Mrs. Minnified would say, "You found it, so keep mining for it. The reward is close at hand."

Harper eagerly studied and played even more intently as Mrs. Minnified watched

Arthur C. Morton

Harper's fingers carry her on a musical journey. Emboldened and growing in confidence, Harper attacked and thirsted for the classical, as if she had been playing for twenty years. Harper was channeling, for sure, Mrs. Minnified's thoughts and energy, seeking heights unknown to her but being very comfortable in that space—as if she were flying through space and time, the pilot was her fingers, and Mrs. Minnified was the engine burning pure truth from an endless tank of the celestial.

To Dance with Angels

Two years and many months went by quickly, Harper continually giving thought and attention to the story of the heavenly angels while she remained busy enjoying learning from her teachers and playing with her two best friends, Anita and Deborah.

But her big day was about to happen.

On her way upstairs to bed one night, Pop-Pop told her to sleep well and dream big.

"OK, Pop-Pop," she replied. She continued up the stairs to bed and fell asleep quickly.

It was about eleven o'clock, and the whole household was fast asleep when Raguel, the Angel of the Order, awakened her. "Harper, Harper, wake up," said Raguel. "You have been chosen, so rise up and take your wings to fly with me to the Heaven of Heavens to dance the Dance of the Millennium."

Harper awoke to Raguel's voice, heaven's royal angel of the dance troupe. Since the beginning of time, this Angel of Justice had been given the additional power of dance and music and of granting children from earth the gift and the joy to fly into the Heaven of Heavens every one hundred earthly years to dance the Dance of the Millennium to entertain the multitude as they waited until time was determined. With wings given to her and taking hold of Raguel's outstretched hand, Harper began her adventure in the heavens.

Harper was so overjoyed that she sang out in a loud voice, "Pop-Pop and Mrs. Minnified, you both were right."

She floated up from her bed through the roof of the house. Up and up she flew, leaving earth's gravity and atmosphere.

Holding on to Raguel's hand, she was immediately enlightened by the brilliance of the stars, which reminded her of thousands of giant jellybeans—round ones and oval ones. They were all very huge. The moon to her seemed void of life, but Raguel said man would someday come to understand the true importance of the moon. Then he pointed out the sun, the planets, and many other things.

Flying, she was as free as a bird. Raguel let go of her hand and called to her to come fly with him. They had a short but long journey to the tippy top and beyond the universe. Oh, how the heavens were filled with colorful things, all working together in order.

Through the universe of the first heaven, she was truly traveling higher and higher with all things passing through and between one another, a whole universe, it seemed, growing strangely in size and shape.

The second to the sixth heaven they passed through was a world far beyond one's imagination, all created so we can forever study the greatness and mystery for certain, these heavens of endless time and glory.

Higher and higher they flew, and as they traveled upward, the heavens became brighter and brighter. Raguel said, "This is the true meaning of light. It's the revealing of the unknown—moving from a dark existence by continually searching and understanding the truth of all things big and small. We're almost there."

Harper was overwhelmed with emotions and thoughts bursting forth. She now had to pay close attention, because they were finally there in the Heaven of Heavens.

The Heaven of Heavens was brighter, more brilliant than all the heavens they had passed through. The luminous intensity of the light was beyond all knowing. The buildings were bigger and far more magnificent and majestic than anything on the earth. Colors and light were absorbed and reflected back, bouncing off everything from gold and silver to marble and crystal. There were precious and semiprecious stones everywhere below their feet, all around them, and over them. "But how could that be?" she asked.

Raguel replied, "The heavens are not bound by anything. What you see is only revealed to the enlightened one who understands the need to be just in its highest form. There's where you will dance the Dance of the Millennium."

"Oh my, no one could ever dream of such a place as this! It's vast and beautiful—the stage, with all its openness. Oh, to dance with all the other dancers and angels here in this place," she thought. "A place truly timeless and empty of everything I've ever been taught."

With eyes wide open, Harper listened to Raguel, the Angel of the Order, and learned the story of creation, how all things were formed, and why they danced the Dance of the Millennium.

"In ancient times and unto today, we dance that which is thousands of years old. We dance in song and thanksgiving for the gift of the holiday. So let's begin our work so we can have you back for Christmas Day, because you will be the lead dancer in your school's annual Christmas Day performance when you return."

"Oh my," said Harper. "What gifts! Why me?"

"Because you have believed in yourself and practiced with joy of heart, but most of all because your spirit is right and your heart is just. We have chosen you to learn from the best in heaven and to return to earth to share your knowledge with teachers, students, and all people."

"Where have all the dancers come from?"

"You're all from different continents of the earth, one person from each continent. So many different-looking faces of all the people on the earth to dance the Dance of Unity, the Dance of Peace, and the Dance of Love—for the millennium and forever more. So go and meet everyone. They all know you, and they're eagerly waiting to meet you."

Harper thought meeting everyone was the most exciting thing in her life. She was just so thankful that she was dancing with the best dancers. And in an inaudible voice, she whispered, "What a joy!"

She marveled at how they all knew one another's names, for it was a mystery to her and to all of them. But she knew them and they her, as if they had all grown up and gone to school together. Yes, they were from different continents on earth, and all came to dance. From Africa, there was Farai, and from Asia, Da Chun. Next to her were Zoe from Australia and Eliana from Europe. Maria was from South America. All of them were together now, and Harper giggled at how happy she was to be there and, most of all, to have been chosen, especially after all her years of practicing. They had now brought her here to join the troupe of the world's best dancers.

All those places that the dancers came from had different names, names of ancient times, which Harper was told were the true names of the places on earth. Since in the Heaven of Heavens there was no darkness, only light, dancing classes began when the crystal chimes sang out, calling all to dance.

To the right of Harper, she saw angels, and to her left as well, and in front of her a great audience of people stood, but she could not see them clearly. She asked Raguel, the Angel of the Order, who they were and why she could not see their faces as she could see the angels' faces.

The Angel of the Order spoke. "You will see them in time, but for now you must dance. It is your time. Time to stop asking questions for now."

She was caught up. It was happening so quickly. Before her was the Council of the Troupe of Angels, along with Raguel, who had chosen her. He stretched forth his hand, and immediately she was floating in midair. She floated, danced, from classical to modern, from adagio to allegro, grands jetés to pirouettes, followed by several tours en l'air, moving rhythmically and with so much grace.

Upon looking down at her feet, she was surprised to see that she was in pointe shoes, no longer in slippers. She cried out, "Raguel, how can this be?"

"It's your time. They are your shoes, a gift from the Angel Minnified."

"Mrs. Minnified?" she said with overwhelming joy.

"Yes, Harper. She is standing over there, next to the Council of the Troupe of the Angels."

"How are you, my precious?" Mrs. Minnified said.

"Oh! Mrs. Minnified, you're here!"

"This is where I live. I went to earth to be your piano teacher."

"How can all this be?" Harper asked again.

"Because the prayers of your grandfather and of all your great-grandparents before him were answered."

Harper then asked the Angel of the Order how was she able to do such things, and he replied that she had allowed herself to look inward and unlock the joy of the dance, which all are given but few seek to find because their hearts are without true love, unity, or peace.

"For the Almighty loves us all, but he does not love all our behaviors. You have loved him and acted accordingly; your joy is now rewarded. So dance that which is before you. The romance of the dance is waiting for you. You've studied the piano to understand the musicality of movement. You have studied the classical movements of ballet and modern dance. The dance is within you—your joy, your dance, your love of all. So dance now, and all the dancers and angels will join in shortly."

As she danced, the faces of the people that she could not see earlier began to shine brightly to her and all the other dancers, for they were everyone's grandparents, aunts, uncles, brothers, sisters, and friends, the known and unknown who had passed away.

The orchestra of musical instruments began to play, yet no one was playing them. The instruments played on their own, magically. Voices began to sing and crescendoed. No one was standing in the choir box, though beautiful voices—beautiful beyond belief—filled the air, singing notes, tempos, and melodies unheard of outside the heavens.

"How can I have so many different thoughts and still continue to dance so differently than I have ever danced in my life?" Harper asked herself. And again, as she continued to dance, even more of the faces that she could not see earlier became clearer still. She could see thousands—no, tens of thousands—no, millions of faces. But how was this possible?

The Angel of the Order said, "They are all who have come before you. They are the righteous souls, waiting and resting until man's time has been determined for him—a time that no one knows, not even in the heavens. So they wait eagerly for the Dance of the Millennium and for the child who will be chosen to dance the leading role, expressing love, unity, and peace."

She danced with joy with all the other dancers. They danced and they danced.

As Harper continued to dance, a person from the tens of millions, it seemed, floated toward her and then said, "Hello, Harper."

Harper said, "Hello, Mother,"

"Thanks for calling me Mother," Pop-Pop's mother said. "I always preferred being called that."

Harper felt and knew somehow that she was her great-grandmother.

"I'm so happy that you were chosen; I prayed for you to be chosen, and my prayers were answered. Your dancing was very special, as if Raguel lifted your understanding above all the dancers who came before you. Time is different here, like the blinking of the eye."

"Mother, how can that be?"

"My dearest daughter, it just is."

Having listened to the stories told by so many older family members, Harper remembered how they spoke of Mother with great tenderness and love.

"Harper, shortly you will return. You will leave the heavens and fly back to sleep, and you will awaken in the morning with a remarkable story. My dearest, two special things I want you to carry home. The first is not for you but for Clifford, your grandfather. I know that you like to call him Pop-Pop. Long ago, when he was about your age, I hand carved a beautiful figurine of him and me to crown the Christmas tree, which you now crown with an angel.

"Clifford wanted so much to crown the Christmas tree that year that he eagerly bounced up the steps and reached out over the railing from the landing. Unable to reach the top of the tree, he lost his balance and fell to the foyer floor, hurting himself and breaking the hand-carved figurine of the two of us.

"His father was pulling into the driveway from work at that time. There was blood everywhere from a cut to a main artery in Clifford's arm, along with broken bones. His father, not knowing what had just happened but seeing Clifford in so much pain, lying there in a pool of blood, immediately used a towel to place a tourniquet on Clifford's arm and then dashed out the front door, rushing him to the hospital. The injury was so severe that Clifford had to stay in the hospital during the Christmas holiday. His father and I would go two to three times a day to be with him. At the hospital was where Clifford promised me that he would never try such a thing again and said he was so very sorry for breaking the figurine that took so long to be carved.

"I told him that I would be able to mend the figurine like new, and all I wanted was for him to get well. I also told him that once he got well, he would be able to crown the tree with his father's help next year. Next year came, followed by many Christmases, but he never would or wanted to take the figurine out of the box to place on the tree. So I want you to tell him for me that it's OK, and this year, I want him to remove the angel from the box. I want him to crown the tree with our figurine this Christmas Day—and for all the Christmases to come.

"For you, Harper, I give my joy and peace that all should seek, for as it is in the heavens, so it should be on earth. Wherever you travel, share your understanding of what is required of us on earth. And that is just to be with one another, to show mercy toward others, and to be humble. Now, Harper, go quickly, knowing that you carry these things in your heart."

Waking Up to Breakfast

Through space and time, Harper traveled back home. Tired from an exhausting performance, she fell asleep in the arms of the Angel Minnified. They floated down through the rooftop into Harper's bedroom, and Minnified tenderly tucked her into bed under several blankets.

Finally, placing Harper's pointe shoes under the bed next to her bedroom slippers, Minnified cleared Harper's curly locks from her face, kissed her on the forehead, and floated away.

Harper woke up to the smell of cinnamon apples cooking on the stove and knew that Grandmom had prepared everyone's favorite breakfast food.

Leaping out of the bed, she flew past the bathroom, completely forgetting to wash up and change out of her pajamas. She ran down the stairs to tell everyone, especially her grandfather, where she'd just come from and how wonderful it was to be chosen to dance the Dance of the Millennium.

Harper, bubbling with excitement to tell her story, burst into the kitchen and said, "Good morning! Good morning! Good morning!"

"OK, Harper. One good morning is enough," said Grandmom as she stood at the kitchen stove preparing breakfast.

"I was *chosen*, and last night I was given wings and flew off to the heavens to dance with the angels, Pop-Pop! You and Mrs. Minnified were right. How did you know?"

Harper's grandmother immediately asked, "What is this little girl talking about? She is talking a mile a minute."

Quietly, her Pop-Pop, having some idea of what had just happened, asked Harper whether she'd had a dream last night.

"No! Pop-Pop, I know the difference. I was there in the heavens. I met Raguel, the Angel of the Order, the troupe of angels, and other dancers from all the continents on the earth. I danced and I danced before a great audience of all the people that have passed on. Everyone—grandparents, aunts, uncles, cousins, friends, so many people.

"At the beginning of my dance, I saw angels to my right and left, and the faces of the people in front of me were a blur, but as I continued to dance, all their faces became clear to me and all the young dancers. I then understood how important it was to dance the Dance of the Millennium and to be chosen as the lead dancer. Thank you so much, Pop-Pop. What a joy it was!"

Harper's grandmother was not quite sure what Harper was talking about and began to ask her a question, but before her grandmother could complete the question, Harper said, "Pop-Pop, Mother told me about the story of your accident as a child and your time in the hospital and the figurine in the box that you never open."

Both her grandparents looked directly at each other, because they knew no one had ever told her about the accident.

Harper's grandmother, now curious, asked Harper to continue. "What else did his Mother say?"

"She told me to tell him that this Christmas Day, Mother wants Pop-Pop—"

"Stop, Harper. You called her Mother."

"Oh, yes. We all call her Mother because she is Mother, right?"

Looking strangely again at each other, Harper's grandparents were all ears now and wanted to hear more.

"Mother is sad for you because all these years you haven't wanted to forgive yourself. She wants you to open the wooden box and crown the tree with the figurine that she carved of you and her when you were about my age."

Right then and there, Pop-Pop picked up Harper and gave her the biggest bear hug. He said, "I believe you, dear."

"Dear Pop-Pop, we both gave each other wonderful Christmas gifts. You gave me the power to believe in myself and to rise above bullying and teasing and to dance with the angels. And I brought back a gift from Mother for you."

"Yes, you did. An endearing gift of a mother's love—that simply asking for forgiveness is enough. Let's go find the box with the figurine that I've hidden away all these years."

That Christmas morning, Harper and her Pop-Pop recrowned the Christmas tree together.

The End

Acknowledgments

This journey of wonderment and belief could only have occurred with the support and encouragement of family, friends, associates, and my editor, to whom I am eternally thankful.

I must begin with thanks to all my family members, for their support was necessary to begin this journey to complete the book and other recently completed manuscripts.

Many thanks to Wayne K. Williams, Jr., my editor. His willingness to work with me through all the revisions made the novel come alive, as well as the other manuscripts. He is no longer teaching English or coaching track and field or wrestling at Saint Albans School in Washington, DC, but I am glad he continues to reach out and help others achieve their dreams as he did with many of his students. Go Bulldogs! Your teacher and coach is still doing prodigious things.

Always there are the friends and associates too numerous to name who share and support one another's life adventures.
To everyone,
Thank you.

Made in the USA
Lexington, KY
13 December 2017